KEVIN HASLAM

You Forgot About Me

Calling
Field
Press

For the ones who came home—and the ones who didn't.

"Should auld acquaintance be forgot,
and never brought to mind?
Should auld acquaintance be forgot,
and auld lang syne?"

— ROBERT BURNS

Contents

Preface

The Battle of the Hürtgen Forest was fought in dense woodland roughly five miles south and east of Aachen, Germany. Most of the major fighting unfolded during the wet, punishing months of October through December 1944—three months of mud, cold, and trees that refused to become cover. The battle claimed an estimated 24,000 American casualties—killed, wounded, missing, or captured—plus thousands more who succumbed to trench foot, respiratory illness, and what the period often called battle fatigue: the body and mind reaching their limit and saying so, even when orders demanded otherwise.

Those numbers can be read in a single breath. Living inside them took longer.

The Hürtgen is remembered—when it is remembered at all— as a grinding fight that offered little glory and less clarity. It was not the sort of battlefield that easily becomes legend. It did not lend itself to clean maps or heroic silhouettes. It was a forest that ate time, ate sound, ate certainty. Artillery did what weather does: arrived because it arrived, shifted because it shifted, punished without malice, and kept punishing. In such conditions, the moral language of war—duty, bravery, honor—can begin to feel like a dialect spoken by people who aren't there. Out in the trees, men learn a different vocabulary: spacing, cover, mud, smoke, boots, morphine. The words get smaller because the margin for error does.

And yet, even the most accurately told history cannot fully account for what the war did after the fact—what it did to memory, to attention, to the private interior life of the people who carried it home. We are taught to imagine the battlefield as a place you leave. Many who served discovered the opposite: the battlefield is also something that follows.

This collection was written in the shadow of that following.

These stories do not attempt to "summarize" the Hürtgen. They don't have the authority for that. They are, instead, concerned with the human residue that remains when the guns stop—what lingers in a man's speech, in his silences, in the way a room behaves after a sentence lands. They are concerned with the small, ordinary objects that become haunted: a photograph sealed in oilcloth; a phonograph in a ward; a pair of boots; a record title that will not release its grip. War does not only destroy bodies. It rearranges meaning. It teaches the mind to make shrines out of accidents.

The title of this collection, *You Forgot About Me*, comes from that pressure point—the way absence becomes accusation, even when no one intended to accuse. It is the sentence the dead can seem to say to the living; the sentence the wounded can feel in the faces of those who look away; the sentence the home front can hear in the return of men who no longer match the prewar photograph. Sometimes the forgetting is deliberate. Sometimes it is simply a function of survival. Either way, it leaves a bruise.

A word, too, about the women who appear in these stories— because any honest preface must widen the lens. The war demanded sacrifice from more than the men who carried rifles. Nurses, aides, drivers, clerks, and volunteers served in spaces where suffering was not abstract. They lived among bandages and antiseptic, among the long nights of pain, among the particular quiet that settles over a ward when a life decides, finally, to stop. They learned to be steady on command; to be kind without being swallowed; to witness without the luxury of looking away. Their work was often described as supportive, as if support were not itself a form of exposure. For many, the war did not end with a signing ceremony or a parade. It ended, instead, in the nervous system—in what the body remembers when it has spent too long bracing.

To include women in this book is not to soften it. It is to tell the truth about proximity. War is not only fought at the front; it is absorbed wherever the wounded arrive, wherever letters are written, wherever bodies are counted, wherever the living attempt to translate horror into something the daylight will tolerate.

These stories are works of fiction. They are not biographies, not transcripts, not claims to particular private histories. But they are rooted in real terrain and real cost. The Hürtgen was not a metaphor. It was a place. People died there. People survived there and were changed in ways that survival alone does not capture.

If this collection has an argument, it is a simple one: remembrance is not the same as nostalgia. To remember well is not to decorate suffering or convert it into inspiration. To remember well is to give it attention—to look steadily at what happened and what it did to the people who had to carry it, and to resist the temptation to turn pain into a clean story with a clean ending.

This book is offered in that spirit.

It is for the men who fought in the Hürtgen Forest—those who were killed, wounded, missing, or captured; those who came home and were asked to be ordinary again; those who learned that the war can follow a person into a kitchen, into a church, into a marriage, into the quiet.

And it is for the women who served alongside them—nurses, aides, and volunteers—who met the war up close, held its suffering in their hands, and paid their own quiet price.

May these pages do what we too often fail to do: keep looking. Keep listening. The needle lifts, and the world doesn't know what to do with the quiet.

Yellow Jackets

November 2, 1944

They rested at the edge of the forest as if the trees themselves had ordered it.

The Hürtgen had a way of making even a pause feel borrowed. The pines did not sway so much as listen. Damp needles filmed the shoulders of the men. Breath rose in thin, obedient ribbons and vanished before it had the nerve to become anything like smoke. Wet wool held yesterday's cigarette smoke the way a blanket holds fever—close, sour, inescapable.

Captain Watt stood with his map folded against his thigh, thumb pinning the crease where the pencil marks had begun to blur. The paper was soft from rain and handling. Everything in that part of the world seemed to want to come apart by degrees—boots, bodies, paper, confidence.

Ten minutes, he'd told them. Ten minutes and then they were moving.

He told Lieutenant Carnes first, because Carnes was the kind of man who took orders the way a stone takes water—without changing shape. Carnes listened with that small, attentive

1

stillness of his, head slightly inclined, as if the words belonged to him already and he was simply collecting them.

"Ten," Watt said. "No hesitation. We go together."

"Yes, sir," Carnes said, and the yes carried no flavor. Carnes's neutrality was a kind of talent. It made him useful. It made him dangerous in a way Watt didn't like to name.

Behind Carnes, Williams squatted on his heels with a cigarette hidden in his fist. Armistead was beside him, jacket collar up, face angled away from the wind. Sergeant Burns stood with his hands on his hips, listening—not to Watt, not to Carnes, but to the forest itself, as if it were a radio that might suddenly catch a signal.

Burns had that slight wheeze that came and went like a ghost. He'd been with artillery before he landed in this assignment— liaison, observer, whatever name you wanted to hang on a man whose job was to translate explosions into coordinates. He watched the trees the way other men watched the horizon. The handset at his side gave off a faint hiss when the line was live, a thin static that never quite stopped—like the war insisting it was still there even when it wasn't speaking.

Gull was farther down the line near the supply bundles, his face bent over something cupped in his palm. It was small and glossy—photograph paper, protected from damp by a piece of oilcloth. Watt saw the tender angle of Gull's shoulders and, despite himself, felt irritation.

Not because Gull was soft. Gull wasn't soft. Gull had the broad shoulders of a man who'd worked with his hands before he ever held a rifle. He could carry more than most and complain less than anyone. But there was something almost indecent in the way he made room for private life out here. As if the rules didn't apply to him. As if the war might pause in deference to a picture.

Armistead spotted Watt looking and gave a short, humorless grin. "He's doing it again," he muttered.

Williams, always the one trying to keep the air from collapsing entirely, said, "Let the man look."

Armistead snorted. "Let him look, sure. Doesn't mean I've gotta watch him looking."

Watt didn't answer. He felt the minutes ticking in his muscles. This was what he hated—waiting with the intention already lodged in the body like a swallowed nail. He had put the order into motion. Now it had its own weight.

He had forced his own hand. He knew that, even as he pretended otherwise.

Watt had been decorated recently—words, metal, handshakes; the bright nonsense of it, given in a clean tent by men whose boots were not wet. "Legend," someone had said, laughing, as if it were a compliment rather than an accusation. Watt had smiled and accepted it because you did. He had stood at attention and acted grateful while his stomach went cold.

Legend. As if heroism were a style of hat.

Now he could feel it: the expectation, not only from above, but from his own men. A captain who hesitated was not cautious; he was suspect. And suspicion in a place like this spread faster than infection.

Watt turned and walked the line, checking faces, checking straps, checking hands that had been doing the same thing for too long. He stopped near Burns.

Burns said quietly, "It'll be loud again."

"Always is," Watt said, meaning it as a kind of companionship. It came out flat.

Burns's eyes flicked to him. "Not the loud. The after."

Watt didn't follow.

Burns looked away, embarrassed by his own meaning. "You'll hear it," he said. "The silence after. Like somebody shuts off a record on a phonograph and your ears don't know what to do with themselves."

Watt stared at him for a beat. The image was too civilized for this place. That was what made it land.

Williams called out, "Captain, you want the scouts forward on the left or—"

"Left," Watt said. "And keep your spacing. We don't have the luxury of bunching."

"Yes, sir."

The men stood and shuffled into motion. Bodies reassembled themselves from rest into work. Packs were hitched, rifles checked, helmets tugged down.

Gull jogged up, breath quick, eyes bright in a way that didn't belong in a forest that smelled like rot.

"Captain," Gull said. "Sergeant says we're short on radio batteries and two belts. I can go back to the trailhead. Ten minutes if I run."

Watt's first instinct was to say no. Not because he needed Gull's muscle—though he did—but because sending a man backward felt like inviting the forest to change its mind about you. Out here, direction itself seemed to have moral weight.

But Watt looked at the bundles. Looked at the men. Looked at Burns, who gave a faint, resigned nod as if to say: better to go in prepared than brave.

"Go," Watt said. "Fast. Don't stop to—" He stopped himself from saying don't stop to look at your photograph, because the sentence would sound petty, and petty was the last thing a captain was allowed to be.

Gull grinned once, grateful, and ran.

As he turned, the oilcloth slipped slightly, and Watt caught a flash of the photograph in Gull's hand: a woman's face, hair pinned neatly, a composed mouth. Not smiling exactly, but not unhappy. Something in her expression looked expensive—Watt couldn't have said why. Perhaps it was the certainty. Perhaps it was that she belonged to a world that assumed it would continue.

Pinned to her dress were small blooms—roses. Or maybe a single rose, broken into pattern by the cheap print. Watt couldn't be sure.

Then Gull was gone between the trees.

Watt looked down at his watch. The second hand moved with rude calm.

"Move," he said.

They went in.

The forest swallowed the company the way water swallows thrown stones: quickly, without comment, leaving only the suggestion that something had entered and now existed elsewhere.

The first hundred yards were deceptively quiet. Damp ground muffled their steps. The trees were close enough that sightlines became guesses. There was no sky, only a roof of needles and branches that turned daylight into a kind of green dimness.

Watt kept his eyes on the men ahead, on their spacing, on the delicate geometry of staying alive. Carnes moved on the right flank, back straight, head steady. Williams kept to Watt's left where he could be seen and where, if needed, he could speak without shouting. Armistead moved like a man saving his energy for the moment it would actually matter.

Burns, with his radio man, drifted behind the first wave. He held the handset close as if it were fragile. Once, briefly, it crackled—an impatient burst of static—and went quiet again, as though the line had reconsidered what it was willing to carry.

Watt's mind kept trying to go elsewhere—forward into the village, backward into the clean tent, sideways into thought. He forced it back into the physical: the angle of the land, the smell of wet bark, the way his gloves had begun to stiffen.

When the first shells came, they did not announce themselves with drama. They arrived with the indifferent cruelty of weather.

A distant thump. Then another. Then the fast tearing sound as fragments cut air and branches.

The men dropped almost as one, trained not by wisdom but repetition. Watt hit the ground, face pressed into wet leaves. The earth smelled metallic, like old pennies.

The shells walked closer. A branch snapped overhead with a crack like bone.

Yellow jackets, someone thought—Watt didn't know if the thought was his or borrowed from the air. A high, angry buzzing, the whirr of something that wanted to sting everything it touched. You didn't hear the shell itself as much as what it made of the world when it arrived: the splintering, the shredding, the shriek of tree pieces flung into other trees.

Men were breathing hard. Someone cursed. Someone laughed once, a thin laugh with no humor, like a reflex.

The bombardment moved on the way it had arrived—shifting, searching for the shape of bodies.

Watt lifted his head. Carnes lifted his at the same moment. Their eyes met briefly. Carnes's face said nothing at all, which Watt found, in that instant, unforgivable.

"Up," Watt said. "We move while they're adjusting."

They moved.

They moved through a forest that looked wounded. Trees with fresh raw gashes wept sap. The ground was littered with green splinters. A helmet lay upside down, filled with rainwater and pine needles. Watt stepped around it without looking too long. In this place, looking too long at anything was a temptation toward softness.

But his eyes kept snagging on boots.

Boots were everywhere, by implication if not by sight: prints in mud, the rhythm of legs, the idea of the human foot trying to stay dry and warm while the rest of the body took its chances. Boots were the war's most constant argument—go forward, go forward, go forward.

They reached the first shallow trench line just before noon. It wasn't a clean, purposeful trench so much as a scar in the earth, dug and redone and collapsed and dug again. Sandbags had melted into the mud. Wooden supports leaned like tired men.

Watt dropped in and felt the trench take his weight like a hand.

In the trench there was the smell of old sweat and old smoke and something else that sat beneath both—decay, or perhaps simply the idea of decay, because no one could be sure what, exactly, they were smelling anymore.

A body lay in the bend ahead, half covered with a poncho. A pair of boots protruded, toes pointed slightly inward, as if the dead man had been modest enough to arrange himself.

Armistead saw it and looked away. "Christ," he whispered.

Watt wanted to tell him not to whisper Christ as if Christ might be listening and offended. He wanted to tell him that whispering didn't help.

Instead he said, "Keep moving. Don't bunch."

Williams nodded and moved past the body, careful not to brush it. He stepped over a coil of wire and his boot caught for a second on something hard.

He jerked his foot free. Something clinked. A canteen cup? A piece of shrapnel? The sound was small, humiliating.

Burns slid into the trench behind them, breathing hard, radio slung at his side. "We're on the line," he said. "Artillery says they can give us smoke. Fifteen minutes."

"Too long," Watt said.

Burns stared at him, then nodded once. Burns was not a man who argued with captains; Burns argued with physics. "Then we go without."

"Then we go without," Watt repeated, as if repeating made it more lawful.

They pushed along the trench toward Schmidt.

The word Schmidt had been tossed around for days like a small, irritating stone in the mouth. Take Schmidt. Hold Schmidt. Schmidt is the key. Schmidt is nothing but a few buildings and a church and a road. Schmidt is everything.

As they approached the forward lip, the forest opened slightly into a ruined clearing where the ground dipped and rose again toward a broken line of hedges. Beyond that, through branches, Watt caught glimpses of rooftops—dark shapes, low, sullen.

He lifted his binoculars. The glass was fogged at the edges. He wiped it with his glove and made it worse.

Movement near the hedges.

Or the suggestion of movement—the way a line of trees could become a man if you stared too hard and wanted it.

Watt lowered the binoculars. He looked at Carnes.

Carnes said, "Could be."

Watt hated could be. Could be was how you died.

"Williams," Watt said. "Get a team along the ditch. Armistead, you stay with me. Carnes, right side. Burns—" He caught himself. Burns wasn't an infantryman. Burns's job was to make explosions happen somewhere else.

But Burns was here now. Burns was always here now, because the war had made everyone into everything.

"Burns," Watt said, "can you raise your boys for smoke faster than fifteen?"

Burns's jaw tightened. He keyed the handset, spoke into it low. His voice changed when he talked on the radio—less human, more code.

Watt didn't hear the response, but he saw Burns's eyes flatten. "They say no," Burns said. "They say the line's jammed. They say—"

"Of course they do," Armistead muttered.

Burns shot him a look, then looked back at Watt. "We can get it when we can get it."

Watt felt the pressure build behind his ribs. The pressure was the war's true currency. It came in waves. Sometimes it was fear. Sometimes it was anger. Sometimes it was the sick understanding that the people deciding your timing were not the people eating mud.

Watt said, "We go."

They went.

The ditch was half-filled with water and old leaves. Williams and two men slid into it and began to crawl, careful with their rifles. Watt watched them for a moment, admiring the quiet competence of it. Williams could have been a different man entirely if he'd been born in a world where quiet competence was enough.

On the right, Carnes moved his men forward in a staggered

line. Carnes kept his head down. Carnes did not glance back for approval.

Watt and Armistead moved straight, because Watt had learned early that a captain who hid too much stopped being believed in. It was a stupid lesson, but it was the kind the army rewarded.

They reached the hedge and dropped.

The hedgerow was ragged. It smelled like wet earth and crushed leaves and something sour that might have been manure. Watt could hear his own breathing loud in his helmet. Somewhere to the left, Williams's men shifted, a faint slosh.

Then: voices. German, close.

Watt's body went cold with focus. He motioned Armistead. Armistead leaned in.

Two men, perhaps three, on the other side of the hedge. Watt heard the clink of equipment, the quick murmured syllables, the sound of someone spitting.

Carnes signaled from the right—two fingers up, then a flat palm. He had eyes on them.

Watt made the decision the way men in his position always made decisions: quickly, with an outward calm that disguised an inward apology.

He raised his hand. A chop downward.

Fire.

The hedge lit with muzzle flashes. Leaves jumped. Dirt erupted. A shout in German rose and cut off.

Watt vaulted the hedge with Armistead, boots landing in soft earth.

A German soldier lay twisted near a stump, hands clawing at his stomach. His face was astonishingly young. His eyes looked directly at Watt, not pleading exactly, but surprised, as if Watt had broken a rule neither of them had known existed.

Watt froze.

In the second that his mind tried to interpret the sight, the war kept moving. Carnes appeared from the right, pistol in hand. Carnes looked down at the young man with no visible reaction, as if the body were part of the terrain.

"Captain," Carnes said, waiting for the next instruction.

The German soldier made a sound. Not a word—just breath trying to become meaning.

Armistead raised his rifle. His hands were shaking. "He's hit," Armistead said stupidly, as if Watt might not have noticed.

Watt stared at the German's face. For a stupid, nauseating instant, he imagined the boy's mother. Imagined a table, a room, a photograph kept dry. The thought was so intrusive he almost flinched away from it.

Then the boy's hand moved toward something at his belt.

Watt's heart slammed.

Carnes shot him.

The pistol crack was sharp and clean. The boy's head jerked. His eyes remained open, now empty of surprise.

Watt's mouth went dry.

Carnes looked up. "He was reaching," Carnes said. "Could've been a grenade."

Could've been. Again. The language of plausible justification.

Watt heard himself say, "Right," as if agreeing preserved his authority. As if the word made the moment less final.

They pushed forward toward the first buildings on the edge of Schmidt.

The village was already ruined in the way things became ruined here—by repetition. Walls stood with their insides exposed. Furniture lay broken and wet. A child's toy, half buried in mud, stared up with one unblinking eye.

Watt's boots splashed through a puddle and he saw, floating in it, a single rose petal—impossible, absurd. It must have come from someone's garden long ago, lifted by rain and carried here as if by mockery.

He stared at it for half a second too long.

Armistead noticed. "Captain," he said, urgent.

Watt blinked and moved.

By midafternoon, Schmidt stopped being a village and became a set of positions.

They took a trench line that had once been German and then American and then German again. The trench ran behind the remains of a stone wall, the stones scattered like teeth.

There were wounded men in the trench—Americans, two of them—lying under ponchos, faces gray. One was conscious, lips moving, whispering something Watt couldn't catch. The other stared at the sky with the fixed patience of a man who had already made his peace.

Williams crawled in from the left, face smeared with mud. "We got the ditch," he said. "But we took fire. One man down."

Watt nodded as if taking casualties were a clerical detail.

Burns came in behind them, radio crackling with voices. "Artillery's asking for confirmation on your position. They don't want to drop short."

"They never do," Armistead muttered.

Burns ignored him, looking at Watt. "If we want smoke, it's now or never. But they need coordinates."

Watt's mind raced. He looked at the trench. Looked at the wounded men. Looked at his own men, pressed into earth, trying to become smaller.

He thought: if we stay, we get pounded. If we leave, we abandon. If we call smoke, we reveal. If we don't, we die.

The choices weren't choices. They were flavors of the same thing.

One of the wounded Americans caught Watt's sleeve weakly. His fingers were cold and slick. "Sir," the man whispered. "Don't—" The rest was lost.

Watt leaned in. "What?"

The man swallowed. His eyes fluttered. "Don't leave us," he managed.

The words hit Watt as if someone had slapped him.

He wanted to say, We won't. He wanted to say, Of course not. He wanted to say, I'm not that kind of man.

But he looked at the trench and understood with sick clarity that the trench did not care what kind of man he was.

On the far side of the village, a new barrage began—heavier, closer. The yellow-jacket buzz rose again, this time inside Watt's helmet, inside his skull. Branches above the trench snapped. Dirt rained down. The world became vibration.

Burns crouched beside Watt, shouting to be heard. "Captain! They're walking it in. We're going to get buried if we don't move!"

Watt saw Carnes watching him, waiting. He saw Armistead's face, pale under grime. He saw Williams's mouth tight with strain, his eyes fixed on Watt as if Watt were the only solid object left.

He saw the wounded man's hand still clinging to his sleeve.

He made the decision.

"Burns," Watt shouted, "get your smoke. Now."

Burns nodded, already speaking into the handset, voice sharp, urgent.

Watt turned to Carnes. "We pull back to the tree line," he said. "We go before they collapse the trench. Tell your men—"

He stopped because the wounded man's fingers tightened. The man's eyes were wide now, fully awake with fear.

"No," the man whispered. "No, sir."

Watt felt something inside him split—something small but foundational, like wood under strain. He imagined himself later, trying to explain this moment to someone in a clean room. The explanation would be words. Words would not hold it.

Armistead leaned in, voice harsh. "Captain, we can't carry them. We can't carry anybody if we're dead."

Williams said, "Sir—"

Watt lifted his hand, silencing him. He looked at the wounded man. The man's lips trembled.

Watt heard himself say, very quietly, "I'm sorry."

He hated himself for the phrase. It sounded like charity. It sounded like absolution.

He grabbed the man's hand and pried it off his sleeve.

"Armistead," Watt said. "Give them morphine. Enough. And—" He couldn't say and then finish them, because the words would become him.

Armistead stared. "Sir?"

Watt's voice went cold. "Enough. So they don't feel it."

Armistead's face contorted, as if he might vomit. But he nodded once and crawled toward the medic pouch.

Williams whispered, "Jesus."

Watt didn't correct him this time.

Smoke began to bloom at the far edge of the trench, gray thickening into white. It filled the air with a chemical sweetness that made Watt's throat tighten—a sharp, medicinal smell that didn't belong in a forest and yet would, later, feel familiar in places built for suffering.

"Move!" Watt shouted. "Move now!"

They began to pull out under cover of smoke, bodies scrambling like insects, boots slipping on wet earth.

Behind them, in the trench, the wounded man began to cry out—not words, not a plea, just sound. It rose and rose until the smoke swallowed it.

Watt ran.

He ran with the sound in his ears and the yellow-jacket buzz over it, and he knew, with a terrible certainty, that the sound would follow him longer than any German shell.

They made it back into the trees in broken order, men appearing out of smoke like ghosts.

Watt counted heads automatically, as if numbers could prevent grief. Williams was there, Armistead, Burns, Carnes. The men's faces were slick with rain and sweat.

Gull was not there.

Watt's throat tightened with a sudden irrational fear. It flared so fast it almost became panic. Not Gull. Not now. Not after—

Burns, catching Watt's look, said, "He went back for gear."

"I know," Watt snapped, too sharp.

Burns flinched but didn't argue. Burns had seen enough captains bleed their fear into their voices to recognize it.

The artillery continued. Trees shuddered. Dirt lifted.

They huddled in a shallow depression. Men pressed their helmets down as if that could keep their brains from rattling loose.

Time became strange. Seconds stretched. Minutes collapsed.

Watt tried not to think about the trench they had left. He failed.

He saw the wounded man's eyes. He saw the hand on his sleeve. He saw the moment his own fingers pried that hand away.

He tried to replace the image with something else—anything else. A childhood room. A kitchen. A face.

But the war had a way of stealing your private images and replacing them with its own.

"Captain," Williams said, voice low, as if speaking loudly would crack something. "We're holding?"

Watt nodded. "We're holding."

As if holding were a thing you did rather than a thing that happened to you.

A runner appeared through the trees—Gull, breath ragged, carrying a canvas bag slung over his shoulder and batteries clinking inside like loose teeth. His face was flushed from the run and, unbelievably, he was smiling.

"Got 'em," Gull panted. "Had to argue with the supply sergeant like he was my old man, but—"

Watt's chest loosened with relief so sharp it felt like pain.

Gull pulled the oilcloth from his pocket again, quick, involuntary, like a tic of comfort. "Look," he said, showing it to Williams and Armistead before Watt could stop him. "That's her. That's my Ginny. See the—"

"Jesus, Gull," Armistead muttered, but there was no bite in it now. Even Armistead couldn't afford to be cruel to something that clean.

Gull's finger traced the edge of the photograph. "She threw roses," he said, half laughing. "Can you imagine? Like I was in a parade. They hit the water and sank. Just like that. I told her—what the hell are you throwing flowers for? She said, 'Because it's what you do.'" He grinned. "Fancy, right? Fancy as hell."

Watt stared at the photograph. The roses were clearer now—pale blooms pinned at the woman's waist.

Fancy.

Watt heard the word in his own future voice and didn't know yet that it would rot in his mouth.

Another shell hit close. The ground jumped. A tree split with a sound like a scream.

Gull shoved the photograph away, suddenly serious. "All right," he said. "All right. Captain. What's next?"

Watt opened his mouth to answer.

The world erupted.

The shell that buried Watt was not the loudest of the day. It didn't announce itself as special. It simply arrived at the wrong angle, at the wrong moment, with the kind of precision that felt personal even though you knew it was not.

A blast lifted earth and wood. The air turned solid with debris.

Watt felt himself slammed backward. He hit something hard—root, rock, the spine of the forest itself—and then the world went dark.

When he came to, he could not breathe at first.

His mouth was full of dirt. His nose was clogged. Pressure sat on his chest like a heavy hand.

He tried to move and discovered he could not. Panic flared.

Then, gradually, breath returned in thin, desperate sips. He spat mud. He coughed until his ribs screamed.

Above him there were voices, muffled, distant.

"Here! Here!"

Hands dug at him. Fingers hooked under his shoulders. Someone cursed. Someone called his name.

"Captain! Captain Watt!"

The pressure eased. Cold air hit his face. Rain fell directly onto his eyes, startling him.

He blinked up at blurred shapes—helmets, faces, the dark slant of tree trunks. Williams leaned over him, mouth moving.

Armistead's face hovered, drawn tight. Burns was there, eyes wide with something like terror.

Carnes crouched near Watt's legs, digging with calm efficiency, as if unburying captains were simply another task.

Watt tried to speak.

His throat produced a sound that was not a word.

Williams said, "Captain, can you hear me? Captain—"

Watt stared at him. Williams's face looked wrong—too soft, too close, too human.

Watt's mind searched for something to say that would make sense of the day. It found only fragments.

Boots. Smoke. A hand on his sleeve.

And roses.

"Gull," Watt whispered, though he could see Gull moving nearby, alive, coughing, dragging the gear bag away from the blast crater.

"Captain," Williams said urgently. "Captain, Gull is here. He's here."

Watt's mouth moved. "Roses," he said, and the word tasted like dirt. He didn't know why he said it. He didn't know what it meant, only that it was the cleanest thing his mind could reach for without screaming.

Armistead, pale with fury and relief, barked, "He's in shock. Get him up."

Watt tried to sit. His body trembled.

The yellow-jacket buzz returned—not in the air now, but inside him, in his bones. He could feel it under his skin, a swarm that would not settle.

He saw, in a flash, the wounded man's eyes in the trench. Saw the hand. Saw himself prying it away.

His stomach rolled.

He whispered again, "Gull," and this time he didn't mean the living man nearby. He meant the photograph. He meant the roses sinking into black ocean water. He meant something irretrievable and small, disappearing without permission.

Williams lifted him, arms under his shoulders, and Watt allowed it because he had no strength left to refuse.

As they dragged him toward whatever counted as safety, Watt's lips kept moving.

"Gull," he murmured. "Gull… roses…"

He tried to say drowning and couldn't quite form it.

But the thought was there, complete as a bruise.

That night, in the deeper woods, the artillery paused long enough for the men to notice what Burns had meant.

The silence after came in—too sudden, leaving the ear suspicious—like a record on a phonograph shut off mid-song: the needle lifted, the room still listening for what had been taken away. The forest held still. Rain tapped the leaves with delicate persistence.

Watt lay under a poncho, eyes open in the dark, listening to nothing.

Nothing, and the faint buzzing that would not die.

In the distance, beyond the trees, Schmidt burned low and without drama, like a cigarette forgotten in wet grass.

And somewhere—whether in the village, or in the trench, or simply in the black filed-away chamber of Watt's mind—the sound of a man calling out did not stop.

Watt pressed his face into the wet earth and tried, stupidly, to apologize again.

No one answered.

Not the forest.

Not the war.

Not God.

Only, in the black behind his eyes, a photograph kept itself dry, and roses fell and fell and fell into water that did not care to hold them.

Auld Lang Syne

December 31, 1944

Tears rolled down Penny Watt's cheeks—cheeks searching for permission, or so she told herself, because the other explanation was worse. She had crossed an ocean to reach her husband and now sat beside him in a meadow outside the U.S. 15th General Hospital in Liège, just under forty miles from the Eifel and the Hürtgen Forest. The air smelled of smoke and cold metal.

Penny had boarded the U.S.S. *Texas* out of New York with no military experience and less understanding. Before she left Rhode Island, she stood on a Newport pier with other wives, watching Merchant Marine hulls nose into winter water, and told herself she would not wave goodbye twice. The Army needed nurse anesthetists. It built programs quickly, trained women quickly, moved them quickly. Penny let herself be recruited because the idea of reunion gave shape to her fear. She ricocheted from unit to unit, slipped into zones barred to "non-essential" personnel, pushed forward on a hunger that felt righteous.

And now she had reached him, and felt resistance as a physical thing, separating her from the man she had come to retrieve.

Captain Watt sat on a crate with his shoulders pitched forward, hands loose at his sides. His eyes were open but unfocused, as if he were staring at something behind Penny rather than at her. When she leaned closer, he stiffened—not with recognition, but with something like recoil.

Nearby, Nurse Maddox sat with a small circle of officers who had been trying to wring a holiday mood from the night. She lingered longer than she meant to, warmed by the attention, by the flirtation that rose in her without permission. When darkness thickened, she stood and moved away, grateful to slip from the chatter unnoticed.

Williams and Armistead were razzing Burns, enjoying the way he smiled in embarrassment in front of Nurse Maddox. Maddox laughed politely and leaned in to rescue him.

"Oh, leave the poor man alone," she said, voice soft. "He's right. War is horrible. These two gentlemen are just trying to get you all riled up." She winked at Burns. He grinned helplessly.

"Burns?" Williams scoffed. "What does Burns know about war? He's artillery. Combat belongs to infantry. Don't you know that, Nurse Maddox?"

"Let's stop talking about fighting," Armistead said. "We've got two charming ladies here, and it's been a million years since we've seen anything but men with stubble. The front stinks, the cold is miserable, the lice are bad; but the worst thing is the complete absence of lovely ladies. For five months with my one good eye, to see two of them—now that's worth going to war for."

"The best thing of all?" Williams said. "No, sir. A hot bath and a fresh bandage. Then a clean white bed and actual rest. There's no comparison."

Burns spoke slowly, with a slight wheeze, as though he needed to ration his breath.

"The quiet," he said. "After you've been dug into a hole in the forest with everything exploding around you—even branches falling sounding like mortar—then you're pulled out and it goes quiet. Magnificent silence, like a record on a phonograph. The first nights of it I sat up and listened. I think I laughed. It was so damned good to hear nothing."

Armistead tossed his cigarette into the dark like a small comet. He brought his hand down on his knee with a hollow thump. Nurse Maddox leaned closer to Burns, eyes bright.

"So opinions differ," she said. "What was the worst thing, then?"

Burns's mouth opened and closed. The question didn't fit his tidy narrative. He searched for a safe answer.

From the corner of the meadow came a wheeze—unintelligible at first, then shaping itself into words. All eyes shifted. The others had nearly forgotten Captain Watt and Penny in the dark.

"What was the worst thing?" Captain Watt said. His voice sounded raw, as if scraped. "The only bad thing is the going off to war. You go, and no one tries to stop you. That's the worst thing."

Nurse Maddox stood abruptly. She had seen Captain Watt brought in bound to a stretcher, sobbing so violently the orderlies couldn't carry him without restraint. Something hideous had stripped him of reason. Maddox feared the look in his eyes because it suggested a diagnosis no one wanted to name.

She touched Burns's arm, voice sharpened with sudden purpose.

"My goodness, the horn for the last truck," she said. "Quick, Penny. We have to hurry."

They all rose. Maddox looped her arm through Penny's and urged her toward the supply truck waiting beyond the meadow. Penny resisted long enough to bend and kiss her husband's cheek.

His body convulsed under the touch.

Penny pulled back, stunned, and saw that his eyes were not soft with relief. They held something like loathing—grim, deadly, inexplicable.

Behind them, Armistead muttered that it was time to rack out. Williams lingered a moment, wanting to offer the broken officer something, anything that resembled kindness.

"You've got a hell of a nice wife, Captain," Williams said. "Real fancy. Good for you."

Captain Watt's head lifted sharply.

"Fancy," he repeated, savoring the word as if it were poison. "Oh yes. Not one tear dropped when I left on the ship, you know. Fancy and reserved. Poor Gull's wife was fancy too. Fancy—she threw roses at him that fell into the ocean and sank, and she'd been his wife two months." He chuckled, teeth clenched against a tide of tears. "'Roses!' 'He-he!' 'See you soon, sweetie!' All so damned patriotic." His gaze locked on Williams. "Do you know what happened to Gull? I was there. Do you know?"

Armistead's face tightened. He glanced toward the medic on watch.

"Come on," he said quickly, "let's get you to your rack, Captain."

Captain Watt barked a laugh that sounded like triumph.

"You don't know what happened to Gull? Well, Gull and I are standing there—two weeks out from that business in the

Schmidt trenches—he's about to show me a picture of his wife when a mortar struck." Watt's words accelerated, dragging the night with them. "It was so far away we didn't even turn. Then I see something black flying toward us, and Gull fell holding his wife's picture with a boot sticking out of his head. A boot. General issue. Blown two hundred yards and planted in his skull. We tried to pull it out. You think his wife would've permitted such a thing? Such a thing!"

"Shut the hell up," Armistead snapped, voice cracking. He tore himself away, cursing. The men shifted uneasily, looking at one another as if checking for permission to move.

The medic approached, trying for geniality and failing.

"You have to go to your rack now, Captain," he said. "It's a new day tomorrow. Hell, it's a new year tomorrow."

Watt's eyes gleamed at the phrase *new year*, as if it were obscene.

"Have to go," he repeated, nodding slowly. "We all have to go. The man who doesn't go is a coward, and they have no use for cowards. Heroes are in style now. The chic Mrs. Gull wanted a hero to match her new Saks Fifth Avenue dress." His mouth twisted. "That's why Gull had to go and die."

He turned, searching the dim shapes around him.

"You have to let yourself be trampled on while the women look on—fancy—because it's in style now," he said, voice sinking into a strangled, complaining slur. "Isn't it sad?"

Penny stood rigid beside Nurse Maddox, arm still caught, unable to step toward her husband without being pulled away, unable to leave without feeling like she was abandoning him again. She did not know which choice was the betrayal.

Watt's gaze found her and sharpened.

"Penny was in style too," he said. "She waved goodbye with

her handkerchief just like the rest."

His arms writhed upward as if calling the heavens to witness.

"The worst thing?" he said, turning toward Burns as though Burns had asked again. "The disillusionment. War is terrible. No surprise. But to find out my wife was awful, that was the worst. To see her smile and throw roses. That was the surprise. She gave up on me. She sent me!"

"But your wife is here now," Williams said, desperate. "She got on her own ship, didn't she? She tends to all of us broken fools with disregard for her own safety."

For a beat, Watt's face slackened, as if the words had passed through him without landing. Then fury surged back.

"She didn't fight for me," he said. "She didn't defend me. She drove me out. She gave me the boot—like poor Gull." His breathing quickened. "Penny has invisible barbs like a swarm of yellow jackets stinging me to maximize agony."

He jerked toward the medic as if he had remembered what medics were for.

"You're the medic," he said, voice rising. "Pull her out. Like a weed. Pull. Pull her out!"

The medic's face hardened. He gave a small signal.

Four MPs moved in.

Captain Watt fought them like a man fighting the ocean. He was wild, furious, determined to stay upright. He shook off hands that felt like rusted shackles. He screamed. His fists swung. He kicked free. It wasn't until the corporal on watch rushed in that they dragged him toward the hospital doors, his cries trailing behind him like torn cloth.

In the distance, flares hissed and burned in the sky.

The supply truck waited to return to base.

One by one, nurses and soldiers climbed in, stamping snow

from boots, pulling coats tight. There was nothing for Penny to do but follow. Nurse Maddox guided her toward the truck as if moving a sleepwalker.

Penny stepped up into the bed of the truck and sat among bodies that smelled of sweat and wool and fatigue. She found her hands trembling in her lap.

As the last few climbed aboard, she began counting without meaning to, the way a person counts seconds in the dark.

"Ten… nine… eight… seven…"

The truck coughed and shuddered. The meadow receded.

Penny hummed "Auld Lang Syne" under her breath, not because she felt celebratory, but because the song gave her something to hold.

"Six… five… four… three…"

Lights in the field hospital blinked out one by one as if the structures themselves were deciding, finally, to sleep.

The moon looked like a yellow-lit ball descending a flagpole, lowering itself without ceremony.

Penny's throat tightened. She kept counting.

"Two… one…"

The truck pulled farther into night.

Everything grew still.

The Needle Lifts

April 12, 1945

The radio in the corridor lowered its voice the way a church does when the name is familiar—low under a film of static, the announcer's consonants clipped and careful as they slipped through a tired speaker, as if the batteries were failing and everyone had agreed not to mention it. Penny Watt heard the pause before the words landed—**President Roosevelt is dead**—and for a moment she thought of her husband, not because the deaths were comparable, but because both were the same kind of sudden subtraction: something huge removed from the world, leaving everyone to pretend the floor was still where it had been.

Inside the ward, men did what they had learned to do. They looked away. They adjusted blankets—coarse Army wool that held old cigarette smoke and the faint sourness of bodies that had gone too long without a real wash. They stared too hard at nothing. Private grief had no privacy here.

Penny sat on the edge of a cot marked by a hanging placard: **SECOND LIEUTENANT PERCY WILLIAMS, 28TH INF.**

DIV. The letters were typed cleanly, as if a tidy label could keep a skull from leaking its life—carbon-copy certainty, pinned to the bed like an order. The bandages around Williams's head were thick enough to make him seem smaller, swallowed by cotton; up close, they had that faint fuzz and medicinal sting—iodine and gauze warmed by skin. One eye remained uncovered, ringed in bruised purple, the lid fluttering as though it could not decide whether the world was worth the trouble.

The staff physician had already been through—an older man with fogged glasses and the exhausted irritability of someone who'd stopped believing in new information. His starched sleeves whispered when he moved, and he smelled faintly of carbolic soap and stale coffee.

"I don't understand what he's saying," he'd told his assistant in a low voice that wasn't as low as he thought. His assistant, pale and too young to look authoritative in a war, stared at the floorboards as if they might offer instruction. Down the row, an enamel basin clinked as someone set it onto a tray; somewhere else, a rubber-soled step squeaked in the corridor and kept going. The radio hissed between sentences, a thin impatience that never quite became silence.

Williams had spoken during the examination in fractured bursts, the words coming out of him like shrapnel: *phonograph... needle... don't let it play...* and, once, with sudden clarity: *Penny.*

The physician had pressed a stethoscope to the man's chest, listened, and sighed as if he were listening to a machine that refused to cooperate. When Williams began to gasp—"A phonograph. Only a phonograph"—the physician pulled back with a small, impatient recoil.

"No use," he muttered, and moved on, followed by his assistant, the two of them heading toward the operating room with the heavy, resentful gait of men who had run out of miracles.

Now it was just Penny, the ward, and Williams's one restless eye.

She held his hand between both of hers. His fingers were surprisingly strong for a man so broken. The grip came and went, tightening without warning, loosening as if he'd forgotten what he was holding on to. His skin felt hot and slightly tacky, as if fever and fear had agreed to share the same surface.

Across the room, a major missing most of his left foot shifted and groaned, the springs of his cot answering with a tired metallic complaint. Another man—an officer with burns along the side of his jaw—lay with his blanket pulled up to his nose, eyes open, listening to the radio's diminished murmur as though it might undo itself and say something else.

The phonograph Williams kept begging for sat in the corner like a piece of furniture no one wanted to claim. Its lid was closed. The horn was dented. Someone had draped a towel over the crank handle, rough terrycloth gone thin with washing, as if shaming it would keep it quiet. Even at a distance, Penny could pick up the faint odor of oiled metal and old dust that rose from its joints whenever someone passed too close.

Penny knew the story. Williams had told it to her weeks ago in a moment when his voice still belonged to him. He had been sitting upright then, propped on pillows, his head wrapped but not yet swallowed, his tone controlled in that way men became controlled out of necessity. He described it carefully, as if carefulness might make the memory less poisonous.

Two weeks after the meadow in Liège—two weeks after Captain Watt's outburst and the long walk back toward the hospital with Nurse Maddox holding Penny's elbow as though

Penny might float away—Williams had returned to active duty. *I can't stay here while the boys are out there,* he'd said, apologetic, as if explaining himself to Penny made it more reasonable. The war did not reward reason, but it rewarded the performance of it.

He'd been promoted somewhere in that time—paperwork, a pair of bars, someone deciding he was the right man to keep other men moving. Penny still could not quite picture him wearing the rank. She still saw him as he had been in Belgium: the steady voice near her husband, the one who did not look away, the one who seemed to understand the shape of harm without turning it into theater.

Now the placard called him Second Lieutenant, and the label did not change what had happened to him.

The barn near Aachen had been barely standing, a skeleton of beams and bad luck. A few officers and men had found shelter there during a lull—if you could call any gap in shelling a lull. Someone had scavenged a working phonograph from a ruined house and lugged it to the barn like contraband. The record they chose was a Bob Crosby side with Johnny Desmond singing, bright as a lie. It had been meant as a joke, Williams told Penny. Something to laugh at in the dark.

You Forgot About Me.

There had been a moment, he said, when the song felt almost tender. The needle's scratch, the lazy swing of the melody, the absurdity of it echoing under bombed timber. Men had grinned. Someone had whistled along. Even the ones who didn't smile had softened, like fists unclenching.

Then the shell came.

Williams did not describe the shell as if it were intelligent. He described it as if it were weather—arriving because it arrived, doing what it did because that was its nature. The barn filled with smoke and dirt so fast it seemed to fold inward, the air turning gritty and bitter with pulverized wood and cordite. A beam snapped loose and struck him at the back of the neck, hard enough that the world went away.

When he came back to himself, he was lying face-down in straw and grit, his lungs refusing to remember how to work. He crawled without standing, because standing would have meant understanding. He found voices—his own men calling, someone shouting for a medic. He found bodies.

And then he found Monroe.

Private Gordon Avery Monroe—nineteen, mouth always too quick, opinions too loud. Penny had never met the boy, but she had heard his name from Williams often enough that she could see him in outline: the kind of boy who put on bravado because he didn't know what else to put on.

Monroe was sitting upright against a section of wall that had somehow survived. His arms hung at his sides. His posture was almost polite.

His head was gone.

Not crushed. Not torn. Gone.

But resting on the blood-soaked collar where his neck should have risen was the record. Intact. Flat and black, leaning against the wall as if it had been placed there. Williams said it was the worst part—not the missing head, but the way the record remained whole, its label still legible in the dim light, its grooves catching dust like fingerprints.

No one touched him at first. Men stared the way people stare at a magic trick that has gone wrong.

Williams said he could not stop seeing the title. He couldn't remember Monroe's face—not really, not anymore. But he could remember those words in their neat, circular obedience: *You Forgot About Me.*

Now, in the ward, Williams's one eye snapped open wider, as if the memory had bitten him.

"A phonograph," he rasped. His voice had the wet edge Penny had begun to dread. "Only a phonograph."

"Hush," Penny said softly, leaning closer. "Percy. I'm here." She could smell sweat under the bandages now—sour, human, threaded with medicine.

His gaze fixed on her with sudden accusation, and Penny felt her stomach fold in on itself. It wasn't Percy she was seeing then—not entirely. It was her husband's eyes on New Year's Eve in Liège: the loathing that had startled her, the strange precision of it, as if he had sharpened it for her alone.

Williams's lips moved. "Needle," he whispered. "It keeps—" He swallowed, his throat working painfully. "It keeps going."

Penny turned her head toward the corner, toward the closed-lid phonograph with its dented horn. She thought of Burns—Sergeant Burns, the man with the artillery voice—talking about the silence after bombardment: a record shut off mid-song, the needle lifted, your ears still listening for what had been taken away. Penny hadn't understood it then. She understood it now, as Williams tried to wrestle with sound no one else could hear.

Across the ward, the major lifted his head and glared. "For God's sake," he muttered, not to Penny, not to Williams, but to the universe that kept sending noises. His voice came out cracked with sleeplessness, as if it had been scraped raw by too many nights of pain.

Another wounded officer—still lucid enough to be angry—said, "We have enough grief with Roosevelt passing today. Can't you make him stop?"

Penny's cheeks burned. Not because the man was wrong—grief was a crowded room here—but because shame always arrived at the worst time, dressed as responsibility.

"He can't help it," Penny said, and heard her own voice shake. She tried again, steadier. "He can't help it."

The men did not answer. They rolled onto their sides. They pressed pillows to ears. They retreated into the only privacy left to them: exhaustion.

Williams's hand clenched around Penny's. His skin was hot, and the salt of his sweat made her fingers tacky where they held him. His eye slid past her shoulder, beyond the ward, beyond the cot, back into the barn near Aachen. The radio's murmur in the corridor seemed to dim again, as if someone had turned it down with a cautious hand.

"Monroe," he whispered.

Penny felt her throat tighten. "Tell me," she said, because telling sometimes loosened the knot, and because she had nothing else to offer. Her voice sounded too loud in the close air, and she lowered it instinctively as a cart rattled in the corridor—metal wheels chattering over seams in the floorboards—then passed on.

Williams's breathing hitched. He spoke in pieces, as if handing her broken glass.

"He was sitting there," Williams said. "Like he was waiting for roll call." A pause, and in the pause Penny heard the small, relentless sounds of the ward: a drip into a tin basin, a distant cough that turned wet and then swallowed itself, the quiet rustle of starched fabric as a nurse moved somewhere behind the screens. "And it was… it was still there."

"The record," Penny murmured, and immediately wished she hadn't said it—wished she hadn't given the image a name.

Williams made a sound that might have been laughter if it hadn't been so close to choking. "Still there," he repeated. "Still playing." His uncovered eye shone with moisture, the lid trembling. The breath that came out of him smelled faintly sweet with medicine and faintly sour beneath it, the smell of a body fighting and losing.

The room around Penny seemed to narrow. The air felt thick with old smoke, old straw. She could almost taste it—dust and burnt wood—as if the barn had followed him back and taken up residence in his throat.

"Did you—" Penny began, and stopped. There were questions no one should ask a man with a crushed skull.

Williams answered anyway. "I didn't touch him," he whispered. "I just stood there. Like a coward." His voice rose suddenly, sharp with remembered fury. "I yelled at him for months. Monroe. I yelled at him like… like yelling meant anything." The sound scraped in his chest; it had the brittle edge of a man trying to force air through damage.

Penny stroked his knuckles with her thumb. His skin was hot, the tendons tight as wire. She felt, in the small movements of his hand, the way panic traveled through a body like current.

"He wouldn't listen," Williams said, and now he sounded young again, too young for bars, too young for decisions. "He kept saying it. All of 'em. Like it was a hymn. Like it was—" He squeezed his eye shut. "And I told him he was stupid. I told him he was—" He couldn't finish. His jaw worked and the bandages shifted slightly, the cotton whispering as it rubbed against itself.

Penny's mind flashed, uninvited, to the meadow outside the 15th General. Her husband's mouth, twisted into contempt. *Penny was in style too.* The word *fancy* slurred as accusation. The way Nurse Maddox had held Penny's arm as if Penny might run forward and be destroyed by it.

"You forgot about me," Williams whispered, and Penny didn't know if he meant Monroe, or himself, or her, or the dead president, or the men in this ward who would be shipped home to faces that couldn't imagine what had been done to them. The line landed like a cold object dropped into her lap—simple, heavy, undeniable.

Penny felt something small and brittle inside her crack. She had crossed an ocean to reach her husband, and still the war kept telling her she was late, she was wrong, she was guilty of absence no matter where she stood.

"No," she said, and surprised herself with the firmness. "No, Percy. I didn't."

Williams's eye opened again. It rolled toward the corner, toward the phonograph. The towel draped over its crank had darkened at one edge, damp with whatever had touched it last. The machine's wooden case looked scuffed, and the brass of the horn caught the ward light in a tired, dull gleam.

"Bring it," he begged, suddenly frantic. "Bring it over. If I can—if I can stop it. If I can make it—"

His voice broke. He grabbed at his own bandages, fingers scrabbling as if he could dig through cotton and bone to reach the noise inside. The cotton snagged his nails; Penny could hear the faint tearing sound of gauze straining.

Penny caught his wrists, gentle but firm. "No," she said. "No. You'll hurt yourself." His skin under her fingers felt slick with sweat, and the tremor in his arms was immediate, as if muscle had become argument.

"I'm already hurt," Williams whispered, and the simplicity of it was worse than any shouting.

His body tensed. His back arched against the mattress.

The cot creaked—springs complaining, metal giving its small protest—under the effort of him trying to escape himself. The blanket bunched at his waist, heavy and rough, trapping heat.

Penny raised her voice—not loud, but commanding in the way Maddox had taught her, the way you spoke to a man sliding away. "Percy—steady. Look at me."

He did not look. His gaze was fixed on an invisible point above Penny's shoulder, where the barn wall still stood, where Monroe still sat upright, the record leaning on his blood-soaked collar like an answer no one wanted. In that moment Penny could smell straw again—stale, damp, packed down by boots—though the ward floor beneath her was scrubbed and bare.

Williams's throat worked. A thin, awful sound came out of him, half laugh, half sob. It caught and broke, then returned, as if his body couldn't decide which sound belonged to which feeling.

Then he said, very clearly, "Penny."

The name hit her like a hand on the face. She leaned in, almost desperate. "Yes. I'm here." She could see the tiny red veins in his uncovered eye now, the way the whites had yellowed slightly from strain.

His grip on her hand loosened.

For a second she thought he had finally slipped into sleep.

But his chest gave a single strange heave, as if the body had tried to restart itself and failed. His one visible eye widened, then softened, then looked past her entirely. The ward held its breath, and Penny became aware—too late, too sharply—of how quiet the room could go when everyone was listening for a life to continue.

Penny felt the absence before she could name it—the sudden stop. **The needle lifts.** And the room doesn't know what to do with the silence. The silence that followed was not peaceful. It was suspicious. It felt staged. In it, the smallest sounds returned like accusations: the radio's distant hiss in the corridor; the faint clink of a spoon against enamel; somewhere down the row, a man shifting and then freezing, as if movement itself might be disrespectful.

She turned her head sharply, as if expecting to see the phonograph's lid thrown open, the record spinning, the horn blaring out the title one last time.

But the phonograph sat unchanged in its corner, mute and draped, a guilty object pretending it had never been useful.

It was the silence Sergeant Burns had meant.

Footsteps came fast in the corridor—rubber soles squeaking once, then twice, then stopping. The yellow-haired assistant appeared first, startled by the stillness, his face already preparing itself for impatience and then losing it when he saw Penny's expression. He stepped to the cot, checked Williams with a competence that looked, for once, like kindness. His hands smelled faintly of soap and something sharper beneath—alcohol, ether, the clean burn of a place where blood was ordinary.

Behind him, Nurse Maddox arrived, hair pinned tight, eyes sharp. She took in the scene in a single glance: Penny's hands still on Williams's wrists, the slackness in the man's face, the ward's hard listening.

Maddox touched Penny's shoulder lightly. Not pulling, not directing—just acknowledging the human being beneath the uniform. Her fingers were cool, dry, steady.

Penny did not move. She could not yet release the wrists, as if releasing them would make the death real.

The major across the room lifted his head and stared for a

long moment. Then, quietly—not triumphant, not cruel—he said, "The poor devil won't suffer anymore," and pulled his blanket back over his face. The wool rose and fell once with his breath, then settled.

Maddox began giving instructions, low and efficient. The assistant nodded and moved. A sheet was found—cotton, clean, folded too neatly—and when it was shaken open it made a soft snap in the air, like laundry in a kitchen, only here the sound meant something else.

Penny finally let go of Williams's wrists. His hands fell to the bed with small, ordinary weight.

She sat back on her heels, suddenly hollow. The floorboards were cold through the thin soles of her shoes. Her knees ached as if they'd been holding her upright by force.

In the corridor, the radio murmured on, already shifting toward Truman, toward continuity, toward the necessary theater of a world that could not stop every time a man's mind broke. Its static persisted—thin, stubborn—like the aftertaste of smoke.

Penny looked at the phonograph again. She did not hate it. Hate was too energetic. She felt, instead, the dull dread of recognition: how easily an object became an instrument, how easily a song became a sentence, how quickly memory turned into accusation.

You forgot about me.

Her husband had said it without saying it. Williams had said it while dying. Monroe had worn it, in Williams's mind, like a label nailed to his collar.

Penny pressed her palm against the edge of Williams's cot as if it were the only solid thing left. The metal was cool and slightly damp where hands had been all day.

Then she bowed her head—not in prayer exactly, but in the old human habit of lowering yourself before something you cannot argue with—and listened to the silence as though it might, if she listened hard enough, explain itself.

It did not.

But it held, for a few seconds, long enough for Penny to breathe.

And in that breath she understood something she had been avoiding since Liège: the war did not only kill men.

It replaced them.

Sometimes with cotton and morphine and folded flags.

Sometimes with a record that kept turning, long after the face was gone.

My Scribbled Leaves

April 16, 1945

Four days later, the silence still hadn't explained itself.

They have given me paper because paper is safer than shouting.

The room is too bright. The windows are painted over halfway, as if the day itself is something a man might be tempted to misuse. A doctor sits across from me with his hands folded, his pen capped, his expression practiced into patience. He has the kind of face that believes in endings.

"Write what you can," he says. "It helps."

He means: Write until you tire yourself out. Write until you stop being inconvenient.

The radiator clicks as it warms, a nervous little machine sound. Somewhere in the building, a typewriter starts up— staccato, practiced—then stops, then starts again, as if the person behind it is arguing with each sentence. In the corridor, a radio murmurs under a film of static, the voice thinning and returning as though the set can't decide what it wants to carry. Even here, the signal behaves like the war: unreliable, stubborn, always there.

The air carries the faint sting of disinfectant and old cigarette smoke ground into wool. Even stateside, the war has its odor—carbolic and damp cloth and the sourness of bodies kept too long in the same rooms.

On the table between us is a stack of blank sheets—clean, eager, innocent. The first page already has my smudged thumbprint in one corner. I don't remember putting it there. My body does things now without asking me.

The doctor is speaking again, softly, like a man addressing a skittish animal.

"You're home," he says. "You're safe. The war is almost over."

Almost over. He says it like a doorway a person can walk through.

I uncurl my fingers and pick up the pencil. The wood is warm from my hand. The graphite smells faintly metallic, like a coin held too long. I begin to write because I don't know what else to do with myself.

This war has given me a companion.

Not a friend. A companion is something that follows whether invited or not.

He appeared the first week I arrived in Belgium—late December, the air already sharpened into that particular European cold that feels older than your bones. The 15th General was built around a meadow, and the meadow looked wrong in winter light: too open, too politely pastoral for what was happening around it. The ambulances came in with their loads and the meadow kept being a meadow anyway, as if nature had filed a grievance and no one had processed it.

On my first day, I saw Captain Watt sitting against a wall facing the iced grass. He looked like a man who had been set down and forgotten.

His left hand was at his temple, fingers moving in a small, repetitive stroke—the way you might soothe a bruise without looking at it. His gaze was fixed on nothing and full of hatred all the same.

I had no business with him. My assignment was different—administration, liaison, movement, a job that was mostly paperwork until it wasn't. Typed orders. Carbon copies. Names on lists. Labels that pretended to be explanations. But his eyes snagged me as I passed, as if he recognized something in me that I hadn't admitted.

He called out without standing.

"Here's the place," he said, voice thick with contempt. "Here's the place for drowning roses."

The phrase made no sense. That was what made it stick. It sounded like a private joke shared by the insane.

I kept walking because that is what you do when you do not know the rules of a man's breakdown yet. I told myself he was drugged. Exhausted. Overheated with morphine and fever and shame. I told myself anything that would let me keep moving.

But the words lodged in me the way shrapnel does—small, invisible, and perfectly capable of killing you later.

Drowning roses.

That night, I could not sleep, and not because of the artillery. The artillery at least had the decency to be honest. It did not pretend it was anything but what it was.

The phrase repeated behind my eyes until morning.

The doctor across from me clears his throat. He thinks my silence has become dangerous.

"Are you in pain this morning?" he asks.

Right now, I am in a clean room in America with a window

that refuses to show the full sky. Right now, my hands are steady enough to hold a pencil.

I look at him and say nothing.

He waits, then writes something on his own paper anyway—a neat word, pinned down like a placard on a cot.

A few days after I first heard Watt's phrase, three war correspondents arrived.

They came in pressed trousers and traveling caps, moving with the casual confidence of men who believed their bodies were protected by their proximity to words. They smiled too easily. They shook hands too long. They had the clean, excited eyes of tourists.

They were charming. They asked after the men. They asked after the doctors. They asked after the "feeling" of the place, as if the place were a restaurant and they were collecting adjectives.

Their jeep had broken an axle on the road to Liège, and someone had told them I could find them a replacement. That was how they spoke: replacement, as if everything in the world had a spare part.

I walked them across the meadow toward a halftrack we could spare.

They nodded at the ambulances. They looked respectfully at the Red Cross flags. They asked if the wounded "kept their spirits up." One of them laughed when he said it, as though morale were a joke he'd heard before.

As we crossed, we passed the wall where Watt had been sitting. He was still there.

His posture had not changed. His hand still moved against his temple with the same slow insistence. His mouth was slack, but his eyes were alive with something sharp and private.

One of the correspondents started to turn his head toward

him—started to look.

Then, as if on cue, all three turned away.

Not dramatically. Not cruelly. Simply with the practiced reflex of men avoiding inconvenience. Their faces swung toward a bomb crater at the far end of the field, and they began to gesture at it with the theatrical interest of people discussing architecture.

I felt heat rise behind my ears. It was not righteous anger. It was something more humiliating: envy. Those men could choose what to see.

"Over there," one of them said brightly, pointing, "that's from the summer raids?"

"Yes," I said, and heard the flatness in my own voice.

They asked me if it was "frightful." They asked me if the Germans "came over" often. One of them said, "Hell of a story," and the phrase landed like a boot.

We reached the halftrack. I gave them directions. They thanked me like I'd done them a favor, like I'd found them a better seat at a show.

As the halftrack rolled off across the meadow, it trampled the iced grass with slow indifference. The correspondents sat high, grinning, their caps in their hands, looking out at the "Scenic Wonders" of a place men were dying in by inches.

I watched them go and felt something in me loosen— something like belief.

On the far side of the field, near a ragged little Red Cross flag, men were gathered in the brown patch of ground that served as the evening staging point for transports.

The brown patch existed because bodies had rubbed it into being. Men sat there for hours, sometimes ten, sometimes twelve, when the trucks were late or full. Men with missing legs sat beside men with yellow fever. Men with arms gone laughed too loudly because laughter was the only thing still attached.

Some of them called their wounds "a thousand-dollar shot," as if a nickname could make a torn limb into a ticket home.

Others stared at the road with the stillness of animals waiting for slaughter.

That brown patch—the way it had been created by need—felt more real to me than anything the correspondents would write.

When the halftrack disappeared, I walked back toward the wall.

Watt had slumped forward now, head between his knees, his shoulders rising and falling as if he were trying to breathe through a narrow straw.

He did not hear me approach.

I stopped beside him and—stupidly, instinctively—laid a hand on his shoulder.

He lifted his head.

His face was not monstrous. It did not need to be. What undid me was how ordinary it was, ruined not by gore but by expression: the tightness around the mouth, the eyes swollen with sleeplessness, the sheer force of loathing held in a human frame.

He looked at my hand on his shoulder as if it were an insult.

Then he looked up at me and said again, quieter this time, like an answer to a question only he could hear:

"Drowning roses."

I did not know what to say. No training had prepared me for a sentence like that.

"What?" I managed.

His mouth twisted—almost a grin, almost a snarl.

"Roses," he said, and his eyes sharpened as if he were seeing something far away and beautiful and unbearable. "All this… and roses."

He lifted his hand to his temple again. The gesture was tender in a way the words were not.

Then he looked past me, toward the meadow, toward the road, toward the trucks and the men waiting in the brown patch, and the hatred returned to full strength.

"Write it down," he said suddenly, his voice sharp. "Write it down for your friends."

I flinched because I thought he meant the correspondents.

But he meant anyone.

He meant the world.

The doctor's pen scratches across his paper. He is trying to keep up. He is trying to categorize.

I can see the word he writes without meaning to show it: fixation.

I want to laugh. The sound catches in my throat and becomes a cough.

"Do you have nightmares?" he asks.

I look at him. The question is so small it feels obscene.

"No," I say. "I have memory."

He frowns gently, as if correcting a child. "Memory can be… modified."

He means: We can blunt you.

He taps the paper stack. "Keep going," he says.

So I do.

After that day, Captain Watt became my shadow.

Not physically. I did not follow him. He did not follow me. But he was there—the way a phrase can haunt the mouth, the way a smell can summon a room you have not entered in years.

When I heard the words front lines, I saw his face. When I saw a newspaper headline, I heard him say it again, with that look of contempt that felt aimed at anyone who still believed in clean narratives.

Drowning roses.

There are words that behave like animals once you've fed them. You let them loose once and they come back bigger.

Hero. Honor. Victory.

Front lines.

On paper they sit politely. In the mouth they become instruments.

I used to think the sickness belonged to the men who came back shaking. The tremor, the sweating, the blank eyes—those were visible symptoms, easy to pity.

But I have watched healthy men—unwounded men, well-fed men—speak about slaughter with reverence, with romantic longing, with the kind of soft sympathy you reserve for a distant tragedy that will never enter your own house.

I watched the correspondents laugh in the meadow.

I watched them avert their eyes from Watt as if he were a stain.

That image returns more often than the shells.

Not because it was the worst thing. Because it was the clearest.

It showed me that the war does not only destroy bodies. It rearranges attention. It teaches people what to ignore.

The correspondents were not monsters. That is what frightens me. They were ordinary men with decent haircuts and pleasant manners and wives who would be glad to see them. They had simply learned, quickly, what they could afford to look at.

They could afford to look away.

Watt could not.

The men in the brown patch could not.

And now, neither can I.

I stop writing because my hand cramps. The pencil has worn down. The page is a nest of graphite smears and crooked lines. My handwriting looks like a stranger's—too sharp in places, too soft in others, as if the pencil has been arguing with itself.

The doctor stands and walks around the table. He does it slowly, as if speed might spook me.

He looks down at the pages, at the long block of writing, at the darkened spots where my hand rested too long.

"This is very articulate," he says, which is not praise. It is suspicion dressed as calm.

He points gently at a line I have written and says, "You understand the difference between then and now."

I look at his finger on my page and feel a sudden, irrational anger. It's my page. My dirty page. My scribbled leaf. His finger looks too clean.

"I understand," I say, "that I am supposed to stop carrying it."

He exhales. "Not stop. Just… set it down sometimes."

Set it down. As if memory were luggage.

He returns to his chair and folds his hands again. He is trying to be kind. I believe that. Kindness does not make him correct.

"What do you want," he asks, "from writing all of this?"

The answer comes too quickly, which means it has been waiting.

"I want it to follow them," I say.

His eyebrows lift.

"The men who looked away," I add. "The men who will go back to dinner tables and talk about strategy. The men who will read headlines and feel proud."

He watches me carefully, the way people watch a stove when they smell gas.

"You feel angry," he says.

I almost smile. Almost.

"I feel haunted," I tell him. "Anger is just what the haunting uses for a coat."

He sits back, pen poised.

"And Captain Watt?" he asks. "You mentioned him as… significant."

Significant. Another tidy word.

I see Watt in the meadow again—his hand at his temple, his eyes fixed on nothing, the phrase he could not stop saying, as if repeating it might drain it of meaning.

I think of the way suffering makes certain images sacred against your will.

Roses sinking into black water.

A record on a phonograph shut off mid-song, the needle lifted, the room still listening for what had been taken away.

A man's hand clinging to a sleeve, then falling away.

I do not tell the doctor any of that. He will only write it down and file it.

Instead I say, "He gave me the sentence I can't get rid of."

The doctor nods as if that satisfies him.

He does not understand that some sentences are not meant to be gotten rid of.

Some sentences are warnings.

When they let me leave this room, I will take these pages with me.

Or I won't.

Sometimes I leave them behind on purpose, tucked into

magazines in waiting rooms, folded into coat pockets on buses, pressed under coffee cups in diners. I do it without planning, as if the pages have their own instincts.

Scribbled leaves.

I scatter them because part of me believes—stupidly—that if enough people find them, the words might finally do what shells do: force attention.

Not pity. Not admiration.

Attention.

Outside the window, the painted strip hides the lower half of the day. The sky above it is a pale, diluted blue.

The doctor caps his pen and says, "We'll talk again tomorrow."

He thinks time is a solution.

I gather my pages.

My hands are dirty with graphite. My fingers look like they've been handling coal.

I stand.

For a moment, before I move, I feel him again—my companion—standing just behind my back: not Watt, exactly, not anymore, but the thing that came through him, the thing that made that sentence necessary.

Drowning roses.

I walk out into the corridor. The radio is still there, still insisting through its hiss, as if the world can't bear clean silence.

The war, they tell me, is nearly finished.

What they mean is: soon we will stop hearing it.

They do not mean: soon we will stop carrying it.

One Good Eye

May 3, 1945

The train let him off like a secret.

Captain Keller Armistead stood on the step a moment longer than necessary, his duffel strap biting into his palm, and tried to arrange his face into something the town would accept. The mirror in his pocket felt heavier than it had any right to. He did not take it out. He had already learned—on platforms in Ohio, in Indiana, in places whose names slid off the tongue like wet coins—that looking didn't prepare you. Looking only confirmed what other people would do the moment their eyes landed.

He dropped to the platform. The boards flexed under his weight. The air smelled of coal dust and thawing soil and the faint medicinal sting of creosote. Above the station, the hills sat in their old indifferent posture, as if they'd been waiting for him to return so they could decide whether he still belonged.

A few people were scattered along the platform—women with parcels, an old man with a paper, a boy leaning too hard on the baggage cart. They moved with practiced slowness, as though the station had become a place where you learned not to rush toward anything. War made even small towns cautious.

At the gate, Mrs. Wells held the ticket puncher in both hands. Her husband, Benjamin, had been a guard here before the war and was now "somewhere in the Pacific," which was the kind of geography people used when they did not want to imagine a body in water.

Mrs. Wells watched Armistead approach. Her eyes stayed on his right side, on the part of him that still looked like the boy who'd once left from this same platform with too much hair and too much certainty.

"Afternoon," Armistead said.

She did not answer immediately. Her gaze drifted left, then flinched back as if her mind had touched something hot. It happened quickly—too quickly to be called cruelty. It was closer to instinct.

Her mouth tightened. "Afternoon," she said at last, and punched his ticket with more force than necessary. The paper tore a little. She did not apologize.

Armistead nodded as if nothing had happened. He stepped through the gate and felt, absurdly, as though he had been granted entry into a country that might revoke his papers at any moment.

Outside the station, the street ran down into town with its familiar slight bend, the storefronts leaning into one another the way old men did when they wanted to gossip. A poster was stapled to a telephone pole—BUY WAR BONDS—the edges curled and whitened from weather. Beneath it someone had tacked a smaller notice: MUNITIONS WORKERS WANTED. GOOD PAY.

He stared at that for a beat, not understanding why it made him feel sick. The words looked as clean as typed placards on cots. Wanted. Good pay. As if the war were an employer and not a hunger.

He started walking.

His duffel thumped lightly against his hip. He moved more slowly than he used to. Not because he was weak—he was not weak—but because his body had learned, in the woods and fields and broken villages of Europe, that speed was a kind of arrogance. He'd been punished for arrogance enough.

On the corner by the feed store, two women paused mid-conversation. One of them lifted a hand in a half-wave that died before it became a gesture. Their eyes went to his face and then away—to the street, the sky, the window display of tack and rope. They did not look back.

Armistead kept walking. He told himself it didn't matter. He told himself it was nothing.

It mattered.

He had imagined this return for months in hospital beds and train seats—imagined Grace on the porch, Grace running down the steps, Grace's hands on his face in a tenderness so certain it might repair him by sheer insistence. He had imagined the town turning out to watch him come home like they watched boys go off: a small ceremony, a few awkward smiles, someone clapping him on the shoulder and calling him "Captain" with pride.

He had not imagined the way eyes slid away as if he were contagious.

He had not imagined the silent negotiation every stranger performed: how long do I look, where do I put my gaze once I can't keep it there, how do I pretend I never saw.

By the time he reached Main Street, his jaw ached from holding itself in place.

A new building squatted at the far end of town where the old mill used to be—corrugated metal, a fresh sign, a parking lot churned into mud by trucks. The sign read:

BOLTZ INDUSTRIAL WORKS
DEFENSE CONTRACTING

A freight line ran behind it, and even from here Armistead could see boxcars shunted along with slow mechanical indifference. The cars were marked with stenciled numbers, guarded by men in uniforms too clean to have ever crawled through hedgerows.

He stood in the middle of the sidewalk and watched the cars move. The motion had the same dull certainty as a record turning under a needle that never lifted.

A woman passed him, caught the sharp trace of aftershave—or the hospital antiseptic that still lived in his clothes—and quickened her pace.

Armistead turned away from the factory and started down the street toward the road that led to his family place.

The sun was low enough that shadows pooled under porches. A dog barked once and fell silent. The town felt like it had learned, collectively, how to hold its breath.

He was almost past the barbershop when a voice said his name with the careless ownership of someone who had never learned restraint.

"Armistead."

Armistead stopped.

A man leaned in the doorway of McGinty's—hat shoved back, cheeks flushed, posture loose with drink. His coat was too thin for the air. His eyes were bloodshot but sharp in that way drunks sometimes got when the world finally stopped asking them to be polite.

Lawson.

Lawson had always been around—an orbiting disgrace—hired and fired from jobs, seen at church one week and drunk at the river the next. Before the war, Armistead had avoided him the way you avoided street corners with broken glass: not fear, not contempt exactly, just a refusal to be cut by something unnecessary.

Now Lawson pushed off the doorframe and walked toward him, smile crooked.

"Well," Lawson said. "Look at you."

Armistead felt a brief, irrational flare of relief—relief at being recognized at all, relief that someone was willing to say his name without turning it into a whisper.

Then Lawson's gaze slid left.

The smile faltered. His eyes widened. Not with horror, exactly. With surprise—like a man seeing the consequence of something he'd only ever heard about.

"Jesus," Lawson murmured.

Armistead's hand clenched around the duffel strap. He could feel his pulse in his wrist. "Don't," he said.

Lawson raised both hands, palms out, as if Armistead had drawn a gun. "All right. All right." He swallowed, then tried again, softer. "I didn't— I mean I heard. Folks said you got hit."

Armistead did not answer.

Lawson rocked on his heels, searching for a way to make the moment less sharp. He failed, which was oddly honest of him.

"They let you come home?" Lawson asked. "Just like that?"

"They put me on a train," Armistead said. "The train brought me here."

Lawson nodded as if that explained everything. His gaze flicked toward the factory at the end of town. "Hell of a time to come back," he said. "Boltz has practically built himself a kingdom."

Armistead hadn't meant to ask. The question came out anyway, like a reflex. "Boltz?"

Lawson barked a laugh. "You didn't hear?" He leaned closer, dropping his voice, enjoying the intimacy of gossip even when the subject was rot. "Boltz Industrial. Contracts. Munitions. Shell casings. Parts. All day, all night. A train goes out every Saturday loaded up with the town's conscience."

Armistead stared past Lawson at the boxcars. Something in him tightened.

"They said Boltz was going," Lawson continued, warming to the story. "Remember? All his speeches. All that God-and-country talk. He got sent off, sure. Came back a few weeks later with some kind of medical slip and a truckload of machinery, and now look at him. Makes the shells. Makes the money. Gives the prayers. Watches other men do the bleeding."

Armistead heard the word other and felt it land.

Lawson's eyes darted to Armistead's face again, then away. "It's a nice division," he said, and there was something bitter in his voice that didn't sound like the bar's usual cheap philosophy. "One man goes away and gets his head cracked open. The other stays and gets rich and tells everybody it's for the cause."

Armistead could have walked away then. He should have walked away then.

Instead he said, "Why are you telling me this?"

Lawson hesitated. He looked down at his own boots. When he looked up again, his expression had shifted into something close to pity. "Because of Grace," he said.

Armistead felt the name in his chest before his mind could form it into thought.

"What about Grace?" he asked, and hated how small his voice sounded.

Lawson's mouth tightened. He seemed to regret speaking at all, but he was already in it now, already committed to being the messenger.

"Grace works at the plant," Lawson said. "Office work. They pay her well. Better than anyone else in town, if you can believe it." He swallowed. "Boltz… he's been friendly. Real friendly. You know how he is with women."

Armistead's vision narrowed. The street blurred slightly at the edges. He could still see with one eye well enough. The problem wasn't sight. The problem was what the mind did with what it saw.

Lawson rushed on, as if speed might outrun consequences. "I'm not saying it's— I'm not saying she's—" He scrubbed a hand over his mouth. "Look. The war takes men. Leaves women with bills and empty beds. Boltz has money. Boltz has a car. Boltz has—"

"Stop," Armistead said.

Lawson stopped. His shoulders sagged as if he'd been holding up the whole ugly story with his own bones.

Armistead stared at the factory sign again. DEFENSE CONTRACTING. The words looked clean. The reality behind them did not.

"She tell you anything?" Armistead asked.

Lawson's laugh this time was low and joyless. "Grace doesn't tell me a damn thing," he said. "Grace used to smile at me when she walked past church. That's about the extent of my privilege."

Armistead nodded once, as if accepting a report.

Lawson shifted, then reached instinctively for his belt, where a hunting knife sat in its sheath—nickel handle, polished from use and habit. Armistead noticed it without meaning to. Not as a weapon, not yet. As an object. The mind latched onto objects when it didn't want to stare directly at a feeling.

Lawson cleared his throat. "You're going up to your place?" he asked.

Armistead should have said yes and kept walking.

Instead he heard himself say, "I'm going to see her."

Lawson's eyes widened. He looked suddenly sober. "Armistead," he said, warning in his tone. "Don't."

His jaw clenched. "Don't what?"

"Don't go in there like you're still over there," Lawson said quietly. "Don't go thinking the war rules apply on Main Street."

Armistead's left cheek—what remained of it—itched with a phantom heat. "I'm not looking for trouble," he said.

Lawson studied him. "You don't have to look," he replied. "Trouble recognizes you."

Armistead lifted his duffel again and started walking toward the plant.

Lawson followed.

The factory yard smelled of oil and hot metal. Men in coveralls moved between buildings with the tired cadence of people who had been told their exhaustion was patriotic. A guard at the gate glanced at Armistead and then—like Mrs. Wells—tried to decide where to put his eyes once he'd seen.

Armistead held up his papers, discharge and leave orders folded into a rectangle. The guard barely looked at them. He waved him through as if it were easier to allow entry than to ask questions that might require an answer.

Inside, the noise came in layers: machinery clanging, a press thudding like a heartbeat, shouted numbers, a whistle. The sound had the same blunt force as artillery but none of its terror. This was violence domesticated, made productive.

Lawson stayed close, suddenly anxious, his earlier bravado replaced by the uneasy loyalty of a man who didn't want to leave someone alone at the edge of a cliff.

They found Boltz in the office building—glass windows, clean desks, a small flag in the corner like a stage prop. Boltz stood with his jacket off and his sleeves rolled, performing industriousness. He looked well-fed. His hair was neat. His hands were clean in that particular way that told you he gave orders more often than he lifted weight.

When Boltz saw Armistead, his face flickered through expressions quickly: surprise, calculation, a practiced sympathy that arrived too late.

"Captain Armistead," Boltz said, stepping forward with a hand extended. "Well. Look at you." His eyes went left, then recovered. "Welcome home."

Armistead did not take the hand.

Boltz let his own hand hover for a moment, then lowered it smoothly, as if the refusal were merely a misunderstanding of etiquette. He looked at Lawson. "And you," he said with faint distaste, "are still here."

Lawson's mouth tightened. "I'm like the smell," he said. "Hard to get rid of."

Boltz ignored him and returned his attention to Armistead. "I heard you were coming back," he said. "I'm sorry it had to be under—" He gestured vaguely at Armistead's face, as if naming it might offend the room. "Under these circumstances."

Armistead felt his hands shake slightly. He pressed them into fists to stop it.

"Where is she?" he asked.

Boltz blinked. "Who?"

Armistead's voice came out colder. "Grace."

Something shifted in Boltz's expression—annoyance, then a thin smile. "Grace," he repeated, and the way he said her name made Armistead's stomach turn. "Grace is working. Like everyone else."

Armistead took a step closer. The office smelled of ink and metal and something faintly sweet, like soap.

"Tell her I'm here," Armistead said.

Boltz's smile held. "I don't think that's necessary."

Lawson sucked in a breath. "Boltz," he muttered, warning.

Boltz lifted a hand, palm outward. "Now, Keller," he said, tone softening into something that pretended to be reasonable. "Let's not do this. You've been through a great deal. People are going to need time to—adjust."

Armistead stared at him. "I didn't come to be adjusted."

Boltz's eyes narrowed. He leaned back against the edge of his desk, the posture of a man who believed the furniture itself would protect him.

"I respect what you did," Boltz said. "I do. Truly. But I have responsibilities here. This town has responsibilities. We're contributing. You know that." He gestured at the window, at the yard, at the men moving under orders. "Every shell we make goes toward ending the war faster. That's the truth of it."

Armistead felt the words scrape. Ending the war faster. He thought of the forest, the trench, the hand on the sleeve. He thought of all the ways faster translated into sooner for someone else.

Boltz continued, carefully stepping around the real subject like a man crossing ice. "Grace has been… invaluable. She's capable. She's steady. She's been through enough without—" He paused, and his gaze flicked again to Armistead's face, and Armistead saw the thought behind it with sick clarity: without being guilted into marrying a ruined man.

"Without what?" Armistead asked.

Boltz exhaled, irritated now that he was being forced to name it. "Without you coming back and making demands," he said. "Without you dragging her into some dramatic scene."

Lawson let out a low sound, like a growl. "That's rich," he said.

Boltz's head snapped toward him. "Shut up, Lawson."

Lawson didn't. "You're going to tell him he's dramatic?" Lawson said. "After you've been on stage in every church assembly for three years?"

Boltz's jaw flexed. "I don't owe explanations to a drunk."

Armistead cut in, voice flat. "Where is she?"

Boltz's gaze returned to him, and now there was steel under the politeness. "Grace works for me now," Boltz said. "She's under my protection."

The word protection made Armistead's vision spark. Protection was what men claimed when they wanted to own the story.

Boltz went on, as if laying down the terms of a contract. "I'll make you an offer. Your horses. The land. The house, if you want to sell it. You can take the money and start somewhere new. A fresh beginning." His voice softened into something almost kind. "You've earned that."

Armistead stared. "A fresh beginning," he repeated, and it sounded like an insult.

Boltz's expression sharpened. "And Grace," he added, voice quiet now, dangerous in its calm. "Grace is not part of that bargain."

Armistead felt Lawson shift beside him. He could smell the whiskey on Lawson's breath, the sweat, the old panic.

Boltz stepped around the desk, closing the distance. "Listen to me," he said. "If she still wants to marry you—fine. That's her choice. But if she doesn't, you leave her alone. You understand?"

Armistead didn't answer. The office noise seemed to dull, as if the machinery outside had been muffled by snow.

Boltz's mouth tightened with impatience. "If I hear you've frightened her," he said, "I'll see to it you're run out of town. We don't need—" He gestured again at Armistead's face, this time with less effort at politeness. "We don't need that kind of disturbance here."

Something in Armistead broke—not dramatically, not as a sudden explosion. More like a bone giving way under slow pressure.

He thought of the eyes at the station, the wave that died, the careful avoidance. He thought of the town deciding, silently, that he was a problem to be managed.

He thought, briefly, of Captain Watt in the meadow in Belgium—the way a mind could turn on itself when the world tried to make your suffering decorative.

Armistead heard himself speak with a steadiness that felt like someone else's voice.

"You didn't go," he said.

Boltz blinked.

"You didn't go over there," Armistead continued, and his voice stayed calm, which was the most frightening part. "You didn't hear the sound when the shells come in. You didn't smell the trench. You didn't have to make a choice you couldn't live with and then live with it anyway."

Boltz's face tightened. "I'm doing my part."

Armistead nodded once. "You're doing your part," he echoed, and the words tasted like rust. "And now you're doing mine too."

Boltz's eyes narrowed. "Watch yourself."

Lawson's hand went to his belt, unconsciously touching the knife sheath. "Boltz," he said, "just—"

Boltz swung a hand toward Lawson—dismissive, not striking—shoving him half a step back. It was a small motion, almost casual.

And that—more than any speech—finished it.

Armistead moved before his mind had time to argue.

One second, Lawson's knife sat in its sheath like a tool.

The next, Armistead's hand had ripped it free.

Boltz's eyes widened, registering the blade too late.

Armistead did not lunge the way men in movies lunged. He did what he had learned under fire, what muscle remembered when thought failed: a short, efficient thrust, low and up, designed to end something quickly.

The blade disappeared into Boltz's side.

Boltz made a sound—not a scream, not a sentence. A surprised exhale, as if he had been punched in an argument and couldn't believe the conversation had changed.

His hands fluttered at his ribs. Blood welled dark and immediate, staining the crispness of his shirt.

Armistead stared at his own hand on the knife.

For a breath, the room held still.

Then the door behind them banged open.

Grace stood in the doorway with a clipboard pressed to her chest like a shield.

She looked thinner than Armistead remembered. Her hair

was pinned back, practical. There was a smudge of ink on her thumb. She was dressed like a working woman now, not the girl who used to sit on his porch steps and laugh as if laughter were an infinite resource.

Her eyes went first to Boltz, then to Armistead.

Not to his face. Not to the scars. To the blade.

Grace's mouth opened. No sound came out at first.

"Mr. Armistead," she said finally, and his name did not sound like greeting. It sounded like grief that had turned into a question.

Boltz sagged against the desk. His knees buckled. He slid down, leaving a smear of blood on the polished wood, and collapsed onto the floor with a sound that was both loud and ordinary.

Armistead turned toward Grace. His hand still held the knife.

He wanted to speak. He wanted to explain. Words crowded his throat and none of them fit the moment.

Grace's gaze flicked to Lawson, to the knife, back to Armistead. Her face tightened, not with rage exactly, but with something more complicated: a hard, practiced fear.

"Put it down," she said.

Armistead didn't move.

Grace's eyes sharpened. "Put it down," she repeated, louder now, and Armistead realized with a cold wash of clarity that she was not speaking for Boltz. She was speaking for herself— for the room—for the fact that a man with a blade in his hand could become anything, and she did not trust the war not to keep moving through him.

Armistead's grip loosened slightly.

And that was when Grace moved.

She snatched a brick from the windowsill—left there for

repairs, red and rough with mortar dust—and swung it without hesitation. Not to kill. To stop.

The brick struck the back of Armistead's head with a dull, devastating thud.

Light flashed white.

His knees gave out. The knife clattered to the floor with a small metallic ring that sounded, absurdly, like punctuation.

Armistead collapsed sideways, his shoulder hitting the boards, his cheek against the office floor that smelled of ink and blood and soap. His one good eye stayed open, staring at the lower half of Grace's legs, the hem of her skirt trembling.

He tried to lift his hand. It did not obey.

He heard Lawson shouting. He heard Grace breathing hard, a broken rhythm.

He heard—distantly now, as if from another room—the factory press continuing its thud-thud-thud, indifferent to human wreckage.

Grace knelt beside him, close enough that he could smell her—oil and soap and faint sweat. She did not touch his face. She hovered above him as if unsure where the safe person ended and the dangerous stranger began.

"What did you do?" she said, and this time her voice cracked.

Armistead tried to answer.

What came out was not explanation. It was a thin, broken sound—half breath, half laugh, like a man surprised to discover his body still wanted to speak.

Grace's eyes filled, but she did not let the tears fall. She looked toward Boltz, then away quickly, as if the sight were a trap.

Footsteps pounded in the hall. Men shouted. Someone called for a doctor.

Armistead's vision began to tunnel. The edges of the room

softened. The ceiling seemed to tilt.

In the narrowing circle of sight, he saw Grace's face clearly for the first time since he'd arrived—saw not disgust, not pity, but something harsher and more human: a woman cornered between past and present, between what she'd promised and what she'd had to do to survive.

Her mouth formed his name once more, silently this time, as if she were saying it to herself.

Then the world dimmed.

And in that dimness, Armistead understood something he had not been able to understand in Europe, something no officer's manual had prepared him for:

You could come home alive and still be carried out.

When he woke, the first thing he noticed was the quiet.

Not the pleasant quiet of a sleeping house. The suspicious quiet Sergeant Burns had described once—the moment after sound quits, when your ear still insists it must be there.

Armistead blinked. His one good eye struggled to focus. White ceiling. A window. The edge of a sheet.

A nurse sat in a chair by the bed, hands folded in her lap, posture alert. She looked up when he moved, her face carefully neutral.

"You're awake," she said.

Armistead tried to speak. His throat was dry. His head throbbed with a thick, pulsing ache.

"Easy," the nurse said, and reached for a cup with a straw.

He drank. The water tasted metallic, as if it had been kept in the same kind of tin canteen he'd used overseas.

"Where—" he began.

The nurse hesitated. "You're at the clinic," she said. "In town."

Armistead swallowed. The memory returned in jagged pieces:

Boltz's office, the knife, Grace's face, the brick.

His stomach rolled.

"Boltz," he rasped.

The nurse's gaze flicked away, then back. "The doctor will speak with you," she said carefully.

Armistead closed his eye for a moment, as if that could undo the scene.

When he opened it again, the nurse was watching him with the wary steadiness of someone who had seen too many men come back with war still moving inside them.

"Did she—" Armistead started, and stopped. Grace's name felt like a wound you could reopen by speaking.

The nurse's voice softened, but only slightly. "Miss Grace Wells brought you in," she said. "She stayed until the doctor arrived. She—" The nurse paused, choosing words the way you chose steps on thin ice. "She's very shaken."

Armistead stared at the ceiling. Shaken. As if the event were weather that had happened to them, rather than a thing he had done with his own hands.

Outside the window, somewhere beyond the clinic, he heard the distant clatter of a train.

A Saturday train, he thought, though he didn't know why the day mattered. A train moving shells out into the world, as if the world still needed convincing.

His hand twitched under the sheet.

The nurse leaned forward. "Captain," she said. "Listen to me."

He turned his eye toward her.

"You're not over there anymore," she said, and the sentence sounded like hope, like instruction, like a plea.

Armistead tried to believe it.

But when he closed his eye again, he saw Grace's face in the doorway—clipboard in her hands, fear in her posture—and he understood the bitter truth beneath the nurse's kindness:

A man can leave the battlefield.

The battlefield doesn't always leave the man.

And sometimes, when it follows you home, it wears the face of the person you came back for.

About the Author

Kevin Haslam is a Rhode Island–based writer and multidisciplinary artist with a soft spot for New England atmosphere and sharp little human truths. He's the author of *Salinger in the Rye*—an Amazon bestseller in American Literature Criticism—and he writes literary fiction that's equal parts lyric and bite. A recovering rockstar (yes, really—The Parker Star Band), he still believes in rhythm, big feelings, and making something out of noise. He's also the co-founder of Yoonie Co., an independent creative studio producing original work across writing, visual art, and music. Learn more at:

You can connect with me on:
 https://houseofhas.com

Also by Kevin Haslam

THE QUIET PARTS

The Quiet Parts is a collection of stories about what happens in the pauses-between decisions, between paychecks, between the words we mean and the words we settle for. Set in a Rhode Island (and adjacent New England) that feels both intimate and unyielding, these narratives move through clinics and kitchens, bars and boundary lines, offices and nursing homes-places where ordinary life quietly sharpens into something else. A young man stares at grout lines and learns what dignity costs. A receptionist at an overburdened clinic tries to help a mother navigate paperwork that behaves like a maze. A move-out inspection becomes a moral trial. An open mic night turns kindness into a performance and cruelty into entertainment. A neighbor disputes a property line until "mine" and "yours" begin to feel like threats.

Written with lyrical precision and an eye for the small, consequential details people miss until it's too late, *The Quiet Parts* explores power, shame, tenderness, and survival-how we carry what we can't say out loud, and how the world keeps asking us to prove we deserve care. These stories don't shout for attention; they do something braver: they listen, closely, to the human heart under pressure-and to the silence where the truth often lives.

www.ingramcontent.com/pod-product-compliance
Lightning Source LLC
Chambersburg PA
CBHW061500210726
48287CB00007B/2590